An ARTFUL Escape

By M.M. Eboch

Illustrated by Sarah Horne

Rourke
Educational Media
rourkeeducationalmedia.com

www.rourkeeducationalmedia.com

Edited by: Keli Sipperley
Cover and Interior layout by: Renee Brady
Cover and Interior Illustrations by: Sarah Horne

Library of Congress PCN Data

An Artful Escape / M.M. Eboch
 (Rourke's World Adventures Chapter Books)
 ISBN (hard cover)(alk. paper) 978-1-63430-395-8
 ISBN (soft cover) 978-1-63430-495-5
 ISBN (e-Book) 978-1-63430-589-1
 Library of Congress Control Number: 2015933790

Printed in the United States of America,
North Mankato, Minnesota

Dear Parents and Teachers:

Rourke's Adventure Chapter Books engage readers immediately by grabbing readers' attention with exciting plots and adventurous characters.

Our Adventure Chapter Books offer longer, more complex sentences and chapters. With minimal illustrations, readers must rely on the descriptive text to understand the setting, characters, and plot of the book. Each book contains several detailed episodes all centered on a single plot that will challenge the reader.

Each adventure book dives into a country. Readers are not only invited to tag along for the adventure but will encounter the most memorable monuments and places, culture, and history. As the characters venture throughout the country, they address topics of family, friendship, and growing up in a way that the reader can relate to.

Whether readers are reading the books independently or you are reading with them, engaging with them after they have read the book is still important. We've included several activities at the end of each book to make this both fun and educational.
Are you ready for this adventure?

Enjoy,
Rourke Educational Media

Table of Contents

View from the Top

1

"Hello, monsieur." Jaden bowed to the statue.

Grace shook her head at her younger brother. But she smiled and snapped a picture as he talked to the figure carved from wax. The white-haired, bearded man in a suit looked like a real person. In the scene, Gustave Eiffel was seated, gesturing to another man. The second statue was of the American inventor Thomas Edison. A woman in a long, dark red dress and fancy hat watched them. She was Eiffel's adult daughter, forever standing and watching the two men. The scene commemorated Edison's visit to the Eiffel Tower in Paris. They were in a small office at the top of the tower.

Jaden turned. "Come on, let's go outside!"

Grace followed her brother and their friend and neighbor, Sophie. Sophie was fifteen, five years older than Grace and seven years older than Jaden. She was hired to look after them that summer. Sophie lived her whole life in Paris, France. Because she was a local, Grace and Jaden's parents allowed Sophie to take the kids touring in the city. She spoke English really well, though she had a funny accent. Mom said it was because Sophie learned English in England instead of in America.

They went out onto a platform that surrounded the top level of the Eiffel Tower. Grace staggered against the strong winds. The floor vibrated beneath her feet. They were so high up that the city below didn't even seem real. Fortunately, a wire cage surrounded the platform, so no one could fall off. Sophie still didn't want to get close to the edge.

They spent a few minutes looking out over the city. Then an announcement came over speakers. Sophie reacted to the French before the message was repeated in English. "They are closing this level because of the winds," she said. She led the way to the glass-sided elevators and they rode down to the second floor.

At the railing, they looked out over the city. They were still high enough up to see far, but now they could pick out more detail. Stripes of green trees cut through the closely packed buildings. Most of the buildings close to the tower were at least four or five stories high. They looked tiny from up on the tower. Farther in the distance, modern skyscrapers rose up.

The wind blew Grace's hair around her face. The whole tower seemed to sway, and she clutched one of the big metal beams. She didn't like being so high, even with the railing to prevent a fall.

"Brr," Sophie said. "Let's go around to the other side and get out of this wind."

They worked their way past other tourists. The river Seine cut through the city not far from the tower. The cars on the bridge over the river looked tiny. The boats drawn up along each side of the river were huge in comparison.

On the far side of the river, green trees clustered around an open plaza or park. A building with lots of columns stretched out in a line behind it. "What's that?" Grace asked.

"The gardens? Or the palace behind it? The Palais de Chaillot has some museums and a theater. It's not that old though, less than a hundred years."

Jaden laughed. "That's really, really old!"

Sophie shrugged. "Not for Paris. Not for France. You come from a young country. Remember what we learned here? The Eiffel Tower opened in 1889. And that was the hundredth anniversary of the French Revolution."

"When all those people died," Jaden said.

"Yes, many people died," Sophie agreed. "The peasants rebelled against the nobles. They wanted an equal vote and equal rights. It was similar to your American Revolution. However, America was a new country rebelling against the British. In France, the fight was inside the country, poor French against rich French."

Grace was impressed by how much Sophie knew about history, American as well as French. Everything Grace knew about French history she'd learned since moving to France a few weeks before.

Sophie glanced up at the heavy gray clouds. "The weather is only going to get worse. I hoped to have a picnic lunch and maybe go to the amusement park this afternoon. There are boat rides and puppet shows. But that will be better saved for a different day. We should hurry home before the rain comes."

A lot of other people seemed to have the same idea and were waiting in a long line for the elevator. The children decided to take the stairs. They walked down almost 700 steps to the ground. Grace's legs wobbled by the time they got down, and walking on flat ground felt strange at first.

As they crossed a plaza, Grace turned back to take a photo. The Eiffel Tower was so tall it hardly fit in her camera screen. The purple and gray clouds swirling behind it made a dramatic picture. The lacy metalwork of the tower seemed delicate and fragile from this distance. They had actually gone up in that, to the top platform? Just thinking about it made her feel a little sick. She hurried to catch up with Sophie and Jaden.

"We should bring Mom and Dad and Joy back here one day," Grace said. Their mother usually taught at a university in Seattle. She was a guest lecturer in Paris for the summer. It kept her very busy. Their father worked from home, writing articles about travel and food. Now he also took care of their new adopted sister. Joy was two years old, but she'd only joined their family a few months ago, after Mom and Dad brought her back from China. Grace was adopted from China when she was a baby, too. Jaden was also adopted, but from within the United States.

They were all enjoying living in France for the summer. With Mom and Dad so busy, Grace was glad they had Sophie. The French girl was more like a friend than a babysitter, and they got to go to many more places because of her.

They entered the Paris Metro, the subway system. The underground trains could take them all across the city. That meant they could visit places without needing someone to drive them. And it was fun riding on the trains like locals instead of tourists. Tourists rode the trains as well; you could pick them out by their confused expressions as they studied the maps. Grace now understood that the colored lines on the map showed the various train paths. She could figure out how to get to the station near her house from almost anywhere.

They got off the train near the house Grace's family was renting. Sophie said, "We will buy some food and take our picnic inside today."

Almost every day, they bought food at a little shop and had a picnic. It was one of Grace's favorite things about Paris. They argued about which cheese to buy. Jaden liked the mild ones, but Grace preferred stronger, hard cheeses. Sophie liked the stinkiest blue cheeses best. They wound up getting some of each, along with some fruit and a fresh loaf of crusty French bread.

Their rental house was in a long row of houses, all together in one big building the whole block long. From the sidewalk, steps led up to the front door of the narrow, three-story house. Sophie's house was next in the row. At the back of each house was a tiny garden, and behind that another line of row houses.

They went in and let their father know they were home. He was in the middle of writing something, and Joy had woken from a nap, so they took the little girl down to have lunch. They sat in the kitchen eating bread, cheese, and fruit, while rain splattered against the windows.

"What are we going to do now?" Jaden moaned.

Sophie frowned for a moment. "I know! We will explore the attic."

"Why, what's up there?" Grace asked.

Sophie shrugged. "Who knows? But the woman who lived here before you is very old. I heard that when she went to live with her granddaughter, and they cleaned the house, they found the attic packed full. They decided it was too much trouble to go through everything, so they simply left it. Things must be very old."

"You're probably right," Grace said. "The attic was so cluttered and dusty we took one peek and haven't been back."

"Wouldn't she just put her old junk up there?" Jaden asked.

Sophie shrugged again. "Maybe junk, but maybe treasures! We won't know until we look."

Hidden Treasure

2

"Hunting for treasure!" Jaden grinned. "I like it!"

They cleaned up their lunch and headed upstairs, pausing on the second floor by Dad's office door. "We're going to explore the attic, all right?" Grace said.

He glanced at them. "Oh, hi, Sophie. Sure, that sounds fine. Just be careful and keep a close eye on Joy." He turned back to his computer as they headed up the next flight of stairs. The final flight, up into the attic, creaked as they stepped on the worn wood. Sophie went first, followed by Jaden, and then Grace holding Joy's hand. At the top, Sophie paused and fumbled against the wall. "I can't find a light switch."

"It's on a string," Jaden said.

Sophie waved a hand through the darkness in front of her. A light flashed and then went out with a loud POP! They all jumped. Someone shrieked—

Grace wasn't sure who, but it might have been her–and then they all laughed.

"I'll get a flashlight," Grace said. "Jaden, hold on to Joy."

She returned with a flashlight and a new light bulb. Sophie climbed on a chair to change the dead bulb. The darkness pressed around them with a musty, unfamiliar smell. The air felt heavy and moist, like an exhaled breath. Dim shapes loomed in the darkness. Grace reminded herself that they were only piles of boxes and pieces of furniture–or better, maybe treasure. Something scuffled in a distant corner. It's only a mouse, she thought.

Sophie screwed in the new bulb and pulled the string. The light turned the spooky forms around them into ordinary clutter. A layer of dust covered everything, and the faint smell of mold pinched at Grace's nostrils.

The bare bulb was bright, the light bouncing off the ceiling. An eight-foot-high peaked roof sloped down until it met walls only two feet high. Thick beams passed through the air five feet above the floor, bracing each side of the sloped roof. The floor was covered with mounds of boxes and sheets draped over furniture, like lumpy squat trolls from a storybook. Even with the light on, the corners hid in pools of shadow.

Grace tried to be practical. "There must be hundreds of boxes up here. Where do we start?"

"The oldest stuff is probably at the back," Sophie said. "I'll bet things got shoved farther back as people added new junk."

Jaden grinned. "Besides, it's dark and spooky and mysterious back there. Let's go!"

Grace kept the flashlight so they could see into the darker corners. "Hey look, we did find a treasure chest!" She shone the light over an old wooden chest with designs carved on the sides and curved top.

Sophie ran her fingers over the surface. "It's lovely. Probably a hope chest. A young lady would

have embroidered linens and things, and put them in here for her marriage."

"I just hope there's something valuable inside," Jaden said. "Let's open it!"

The chest didn't even have a lock, but the lid stuck. Sophie and Jaden pried at it while Grace held the flashlight and Joy's hand. Finally it creaked open. Jaden clapped. "We got it!"

They peered inside the box. The flashlight played over folded cloth, spotted and stained. Then the smell of mold hit them.

"Ugh!" They jerked back and Sophie slammed down the lid. They moved away from the chest, hands over their mouths and noses. Jaden coughed. "So much for a treasure chest."

"I guess that's what happens when you leave a wooden chest in a damp attic for so long," Sophie said. "It's too bad. Some girl probably put a lot of work into those."

"Now what?" Grace frowned at a broken chair. "How do we know what's valuable, anyway?"

"We look for the oldest stuff, right?" Jaden said.

"It's not that easy," Sophie said. "Age isn't as

important as how rare it is. People will collect anything, from stamps and coins to comic books and movie posters. So say there's a new comic series, and they only print a thousand copies of the first issue, because they don't know how popular it will be. But then it gets really popular. The collectors all want that first issue. But by that time, most of those thousand copies have been thrown away or damaged."

She gestured at the boxes piled around them. "Or hidden away in an attic. Lost. So if you have one of the first copies, in good condition, it's worth a lot of money. But if they printed a million copies of something, then it doesn't matter if you have one in perfect condition. It's worthless."

Grace grimaced. "So basically you have to be an expert and know about all this stuff."

"They have books to help you identify things and what they are worth," Sophie said.

"Sounds like a lot of work," Jaden said.

Sophie grinned at him. "Did you expect treasure hunting to be easy?"

They found some toys for Joy to play with while they searched. They kept at it for a couple of hours, unearthing boxes of old magazines, more moldy clothes, and a cool roll-top desk. They checked all the drawers and pigeon holes in the desk. It was empty except for a few pencils and faded scraps of paper. They even looked for secret drawers but didn't find any.

Rain drummed on the roof. Joy got tired, so Grace took her downstairs for a nap. When Grace went back upstairs, Sophie was standing in the middle of the room looking up. It took Grace a moment to see Jaden. He was standing on one of the cross beams that braced each side of the sloped roof.

"Jaden, what are you doing?"

"Sophie noticed that the ceiling looks different here." He stepped across two feet of open air to the next wooden beam.

"It's all right; I'll spot him, like in gymnastics." Sophie was one of the top gymnasts in the country. She had been teaching Grace and Jaden some tumbling. Grace was good at somersaults and cartwheels, and she was working on a walkover. Jaden at first thought gymnastics was too girly. He'd changed his mind after watching videos of the men's

Olympic gymnastics team. And he loved anything that took him up off the ground.

Sophie held her arms out loosely, moving under Jaden as he moved. "If he comes off, I will break the fall. It is just like the balance beam, no?"

Except the balance beam wasn't so high, and they'd had padded mats underneath in case they fell. Grace suspected that Sophie was not quite as responsible as Grace's parents thought. Mom and Dad didn't know what Sophie let them do sometimes. If they had, they might have hired a different babysitter. But Grace and Jaden weren't about to tell and ruin the fun.

Jaden walked along the beam toward the sloped ceiling. He tapped a square section. It looked lighter than the area around it, as if the ceiling had been repaired. "I think it's a secret door!" A moment later it swung open, revealing a space about two feet square. "There's something inside." Jaden pulled out a package and stood up. He wobbled, arms waving. "Oh no, I'm going to fall!"

"Jaden!" Grace rushed forward, but by the time she reached Sophie's side, Jaden was sitting on the roof beam, laughing.

"Got you!"

"It's not funny," Grace said, but a moment later she decided maybe it was. Falling for his trick was better than having him really fall. She and Jaden fought a lot at home, but they were getting along better in France. When you didn't have anyone else to play with, you learned to make peace.

Sophie helped Jaden down from the beam and they looked at the package he was holding. The covering was some kind of fabric with a waxy texture. "Why would anyone hide it up there?" Sophie asked. They went to the brightest spot in the attic and brushed off a box. Sophie carefully unwrapped the package. Inside was a painting of a woman. She seemed to be gazing back at them. "It's beautiful," Grace said.

Sophie nodded. "But why was it hidden in the ceiling?" She bent closer to the painting and peered at the corner. "The painter signed only with his initials."

"Is that RL?" Grace asked. "Or RHL?" She studied the initials a moment longer. "Or PHL?"

Sophie straightened and smiled. "I think we may have found our treasure, and a mystery as well."

WORTH a FORTUNE?

3

They agreed not to tell their parents right away. It would be more fun to solve the mystery themselves. To do that, Sophie suggested they visit a museum the next day. By studying other paintings, maybe they could learn something about this one. Grace and Jaden's parents were delighted when they expressed interest in visiting a museum. Their father went online and ordered tickets to the Louvre. "It's probably the most famous museum in the world," he said.

They took the Metro the next morning. After getting off the subway, they walked across a large plaza. Buildings several stories high, with lots of arches and windows, surrounded the plaza on three sides. The fancy buildings were all part of the museum. "It would take months to see the whole Louvre," Sophie said, "but we only need to find the right gallery."

"The what?" Jaden asked.

"A gallery is a room for showing art," Sophie said. "The museum has many galleries for different kinds of art. We have a painting, not a sculpture, so we may ignore the sculpture galleries. The painting is certainly European, so we do not need to visit the Egyptian gallery."

"Egypt would be cool, though," Jaden commented.

"True. We may go another time. Today we have a mission! I did some research last night," Sophie said. "Rembrandt signed his paintings in different ways over the years. At one time he used the initials RHL, close together so it's hard to read. I found a picture online and it looks like our signature."

"Is that good?" Jaden asked.

"Rembrandt is a very famous artist. If the painting is his, it is worth a lot of money."

Jaden grinned. "That is good!"

They moved past groups of people, many taking photos. A few street performers danced or played music. A woman wearing black and white did a mime, acting out a scene with exaggerated gestures but no words. In the middle of the plaza stood a glass pyramid as high as a two-story house.

"We can go in at the pyramid," Sophie said.

Inside the pyramid, a spiral staircase circled down to a lower level. At the bottom they paused, looking up at the pyramid above them. Glass panels framed in black showed the blue sky above.

People waited in long lines to buy tickets. Good thing they already had theirs! At the information desk, Sophie asked, "Where are the Rembrandt paintings?"

"The Rembrandt room is in the Richelieu wing, second floor, room number 31." The woman unfolded a brochure and circled something on a map.

Sophie thanked her and walked away. "First, though, we must visit the Mona Lisa, because your parents will expect it and ask you about it." She glanced at the brochure as she walked through the crowds, holding Jaden's hand so he wouldn't dash off. "The Louvre was built around 1200 CE. It was a fortress and later a royal palace. After the French Revolution, it became a museum."

She winked at Grace. "We want your parents to

think you are having an educational summer."

Simply living in another country was a big education. But since Mom was a history professor, she would be pleased if the children learned some history. Grace didn't think she could remember the dates, but she murmured, "Fort, palace, museum. And really, really old, as Jaden would say."

Within minutes, Grace was completely lost, but Sophie seemed to know where she was going. They entered a large room with a high ceiling. Paintings hung close together on the side walls. Sophie led the way through the crowd, squirming toward the far end of the room. Surrounded by taller grownups, Grace couldn't see anything on the wall, but many people held cameras over their heads pointing that way.

Finally they got close enough to see one painting displayed all by itself. It showed the head and upper body of a woman with her hands crossed in front of her. She had dark hair and a dark dress.

"There is the famous smile," Sophie said. "People ask why she was smiling. Is she happy or sad? It is a mystery that may never be solved."

The woman's mouth was closed, but the corners

of her lips turned up slightly. "She looks like she's tired of sitting there," Grace said.

Sophie chuckled. "That may be it. Sitting for a painting would take hours, and it is hard enough to smile naturally for a photo. Well, you may tell your parents you have seen it. Let's go." She spun and pushed back through the crowd.

It took them 15 minutes to get to the Rembrandt gallery. The room held large paintings, some of them twice as tall as a person. Most were scenes from the Bible or history. Smaller paintings were often portraits of people. There were sketches, too—rough drawings in ink.

The group focused on the portraits. "Why did he paint that same guy so much?" Jaden asked.

Sophie checked the tag under a portrait of a man with curly brown hair and a puffy black hat. "That is Rembrandt himself. He painted many self-portraits. And if our painting was a self-portrait, it would make our work easier. But who the woman in the painting is, we do not know." She tipped her head to the side and frowned as she studied the painting. "The style does look the same, though."

"I think so too," Grace said. "What about the signature? This one isn't right—he wrote out his whole name."

They looked at some other paintings and finally found one with the RHL initials. Sophie brought up a photo of their painting on her phone. She zoomed in on the initials. "It looks pretty close," Grace said.

Sophie nodded. "But of course it could be a forgery—a fake. Or someone else might have used a similar mark."

"So we still don't know anything?" Jaden asked, "Why didn't you just look at the paintings online instead of dragging us here?"

Sophie lifted her chin. "You must see art in person to truly appreciate it. A photograph of a painting tells you very little."

Jaden looked at Grace and rolled his eyes. She gave a little shrug. It was different to see a statue in person than a flat picture of the statue. And being around famous old paintings made her feel more grown up.

Grace looked at some of the labels on the paintings. "These are really old—from the 1600s! Could we truly have found something almost 400 years old? How will we know for sure?"

"We may have to talk to an expert," Sophie said. "But if this is a real Rembrandt painting, it is very valuable."

"How much money would it be worth?" Jaden asked.

Sophie glanced around as if checking whether anyone was listening. She leaned closer and whispered, "More than you can possibly imagine."

Jaden's eyes got big and he grinned.

"It doesn't belong to us, though," Grace said.

"Finders keepers!" Jaden said.

"I'm not sure it works that way," Grace said. "It was in the house we were renting, not something we found on the street. If we took the kitchen table with us when we left, that would be stealing."

"But the painting was hidden," Jaden insisted. "Probably for years and years and years. Whoever put it there must have forgotten about it. Or he's dead!" Jaden looked pleased at that idea.

Sophie shook her head. "We will talk about that later. I must think of how to find a Rembrandt expert.

Shall we visit the Egyptian rooms while we are here?"

They agreed. But while Grace was looking at statues and wall carvings and mummy coffins, her mind went over the possibilities. Had they really found a valuable painting by a famous painter? And if so, what would they do about it?

Tales of Death and Danger

4

By the time they returned home, they were worn out from their long day. Sophie said goodbye and Grace and Jaden played with Joy for a while. Then Grace helped her father make dinner. Dad wanted to learn French cooking, so they made a traditional French dish. They cut up apples and leeks and roasted them with chicken.

Over dinner, Jaden asked, "What would you do if you found a treasure?"

Grace shot him a look. They were supposed to keep it secret! But Dad just chuckled and said, "I suppose it would depend on the treasure. Did you see a lot of cool stuff at the museum?"

Jaden nodded. Before he could give away anything, Grace said, "The Egyptian stuff is cool. And we saw that smiling lady, Mona Lisa."

"Oh, what did you think of the mysterious smile?"

Mom asked.

Jaden said, "She looked like she needed to go to the bathroom."

Mom chuckled. "Well, Dad and I still need to make sure we see her in person. I've seen so many pictures, but they're not the same."

Huh, that was sort of what Sophie said, Grace thought. She nibbled on a chicken leg. The roasted apples added sweetness and the leeks tasted like mild onions.

Grace wanted to tell their parents about the painting, but it was fun having a secret. Maybe she could learn something without giving away too much. One question was how long the painting had been hidden in the attic. "Mom, do you know how old this house is?"

"About 150 years, but it's been renovated since then. Good thing, or we wouldn't have running water and toilets that flush! Actually, this house has an interesting history." Since Mom was a history professor, it made sense that she researched their house. "Some of it is sad, though. How much do you know about World War II?"

"That was when Hitler tried to take over and killed all those people, right? Wait, that wasn't part of the French Revolution, was it?"

"No, the French Revolution was from 1787 to 1799. World War II started in Europe in the 1930s." Mom thought for a moment. "It's complicated, and you'll learn more about it in high school. But basically, the Germans were trying to take over Europe. They invaded France in 1940. Many Jewish people lived in Paris. Hitler didn't like the Jews."

"Why not?" Jaden asked.

"Actually, he didn't like a lot of people. He thought anyone different was bad. He convinced a lot of Germans that Jews were bad."

Dad said, "When times are tough, when people have trouble finding work, or there's not enough money, a lot of people look for someone to blame. Most often they look for someone who's different. A different race, a different religion, whatever. It doesn't matter if there's a reason to blame those people. It's easier to blame others than take responsibility."

Mom nodded. "The Nazis sent millions of people to prison camps, including several million Jews. Many people died in those camps. Some Jews fled to other countries to avoid arrest. Others who couldn't escape went into hiding. Many joined the Resistance, a group that spied on and fought against the Germans. I won't go into detail, not over dinner." Mom looked sad.

Grace hadn't expected her question to lead to talk of war and death. "What about our house?"

"Oh, right. A lot of Jews lived in this part of the city. Two families wound up hiding in the attic here for more than a year. You might have heard of Anne Frank. She was a Jewish girl who wrote a diary about hiding in an attic with her family during the war. That was in Amsterdam. But many people went into hiding. The families here were eventually found and arrested, and sent to the prison camps."

Mom gave Grace a curious look. "That's right, you were exploring the attic yesterday. Do you suppose those families left anything there? They wouldn't have been able to take much with them. And even if they survived the war, they might not have come back here."

Could the painting have been hidden by Jewish people before they were arrested? If it was valuable, they might want to save it until they came back. And maybe they never did come back to claim it.

Of course, Grace didn't know who had left the painting, or when. She said only, "A lot of the stuff up there isn't in good shape."

"No, I suppose not. It's a shame how many valuable records get lost. Even a young girl's diary can tell us so much about the past. Historians wish we could preserve everything forever!" Mom got up. "I stopped at a bakery and got some fruit tarts for dessert. Who wants one?"

The whole family chorused, "Me!"

After dinner, Grace ran next door to tell Sophie what she'd learned. The older girl nodded. "That would explain hiding the painting. The Nazis stole many works of art. The ones Hitler liked went to Germany. They took many thousands of paintings and other artworks. Even today you hear stories about people trying to reclaim the art their grandparents lost."

"Does that mean the painting belongs to the family that hid in our attic? If anybody is left, that is."

Sophie nodded. "It might be difficult to find them and prove what happened. We shall see. But first we need to know if it is a real painting, or a fake. Or it could be by some other artist and not worth so much."

"How do we find out?" Grace asked.

"Tomorrow we will go to an art gallery. We will find an expert and asked some questions."

"Should we take the painting with us?"

"No, keep it hidden," Sophie said. "If it is a Rembrandt, many people will want to steal it."

Grace walked the few steps back to her front door. She paused on her stoop and looked down the street. It was quiet, with only a few people walking in the distance. It was hard to imagine the fear and violence that had been here.

She hoped finding the painting wouldn't bring more danger.

A Suspicious Expert

5

The next morning, Sophie took Grace and Jaden to find an expert. "I found this art gallery online," Sophie said. "The website says they buy family heirlooms."

"What's a ... the thing you said?" Jaden asked. Grace was glad she didn't have to ask.

"An heirloom is a family treasure. If your family owned a painting for many years, it might be an heirloom. If people bring their treasures to this gallery, someone there must know how to judge the value. They also specialize in old paintings. Some galleries only sell new work by modern artists. We need a place that knows about artists from the past."

"It sounds like they should have our expert," Grace said.

The gallery was in an old neighborhood. Its sign needed a new coat of paint. A bell on the door jingled as they entered a dim, cluttered room. Paintings hung on the wall, but they also sat on the floor, leaning against the wall. Music came from a back room, where the light was brighter. As they walked toward that door, Grace glimpsed someone sitting at a table. The young man had on strange, thick glasses and was leaning over a painting. He dipped a brush into a small dish and dabbed at the painting.

A woman with orange hair and dark eye makeup hurried out of the room and closed the door behind her. Her smile faded when she saw the children. She said something in French and then switched to English. "What do you want? No public bathrooms here."

Sophie put on a haughty grownup look and greeted the woman in French. Then she switched to English so Grace and Jaden could understand. "We need to know how to tell if an old painting is real."

The woman went behind a counter and sat on a stool. "I don't have time to help you with class projects. This is a business."

Grace might have backed down from the rudeness, but Sophie plowed ahead. "It is a business question.

Do you not buy family heirlooms? You must know how to judge the real from the fake."

The woman looked more interested. "Do you children have something to sell?"

Sophie shrugged. "Perhaps."

The woman studied them for a moment. Her voice became friendlier. "I would like to help you, but you must tell me exactly what you have. May I offer you a cup of coffee while we discuss the matter?"

"Coffee for me," Sophie said, "but not for the children."

"Perhaps I have some lemonade." The woman disappeared into the back room.

Jaden said, "I don't like her."

"Shh!" Sophie warned. She whispered, "She does not take us seriously because we are young. We must convince her we have something she may want."

"She's going to want to see the painting," Grace said.

"Yes, but we will not let her, not yet. If she thinks we are foolish children, she may try to cheat us." Sophie pulled out her phone. "Let's not tell her too much, but I can show her the photo. Then she will know we are serious."

The woman came out with two cups, and two bottled drinks, on a silver tray. "You may call me Madame Estelle. Now tell me about yourselves. I can tell that you are French." She gave Sophie one of the cups and handed the bottles to Grace and Jaden. "And you two are Americans?"

Grace nodded. "My brother and I are in Paris for the summer. I'm Grace and he's Jaden."

"And your family name?"

Before Grace could tell her last name, Sophie broke in. "I am Sophie. We are investigating something we found." She held out her phone with the photo of the painting showing.

The woman studied it for a long time. She looked at the close-up photo Sophie had taken of the initials. Sophie drank her coffee while Grace and Jaden sipped at their fizzy lemonade. Finally the woman handed back the phone. "It is certainly a fake."

Grace sighed and Jaden groaned. Sophie asked, "How can you tell from a photo?"

"The signs are there." She took a sip from her cup. "However, even a fake has some value. It appears to

be in good condition. I will give you 100 euros for it."

"Really?" Jaden perked up, and then looked confused. "Wait, is that a lot of money?"

The woman leaned forward. "You can buy many toys and games for 100 euros. When can you bring me the painting?"

Sophie put down her coffee cup and backed toward the door. "We will think about it."

"Wait," the woman said. "Leave me your address and phone number."

"We will return if we decide to sell the painting," Sophie said. "But I think we will ask for a second opinion first."

The woman frowned. "I can see you are a smart businesswoman. I know the expert to ask. Go out to Versailles tomorrow. You can take a bus or train there. Ask for Monsieur Dubois at the renovation workshop. He will tell you all you need to know, but you must take the painting with you. He will want to test it. And if you do decide to sell, please come to me first."

"Thank you for your time," Sophie said with a nod.

Outside, Grace asked, "A hundred euros isn't really

that much money, is it? Euros are about the same as dollars." The euro was the money used throughout much of Europe.

"That's right," Sophie said. "The exchange rate varies, so sometimes you can buy more dollars with euros, and sometimes less. If this is a real Rembrandt, it should be worth millions. An old painting by a less famous artist should be worth thousands. Her price seems low even for a fake. But no doubt she thought to take advantage of us because we are young."

Something jingled behind them—the sound of the bell over the shop door. Sophie pulled them into an alley and peeked back around the corner. "The man from the back room has come out. He is looking around. Is he looking for us?" A moment later, she said, "He has gone back inside. I don't think I trust that gallery."

They cut through the alley to another street. "Now what?" Grace asked. "Do we go to that place she said?"

"I think so," Sophie said. "Versailles is a very famous palace. Now it is a museum, and you should see it anyway. But perhaps we will not take the painting with us until after we have spoken to Monsieur Dubois. It will stay safe hidden in your attic."

"This is exciting!" Jaden said. "I thought an art gallery would be boring, but it was creepy. That woman was weird. I don't think she likes kids."

"Yeah, she acted sweet but it seemed fake," Grace agreed. "Some people are uncomfortable around kids. Maybe that's why she seemed so... ." She couldn't think of the right word.

"Something is not right," Sophie said. "We must be careful with Monsieur Dubois as well. He may be working with that woman."

"Then why are we going to see him at all?" Grace asked.

Sophie grinned. "Because it is all so exciting and entertaining! Like being in a movie."

Jaden nodded. "This is fun."

"Except for the part about how the painting might have belonged to Jews killed by the Nazis," Grace said.

"That part is very sad," Sophie agreed. "But if we find out the truth, we can help right a wrong from the past."

"We'll be heroes!" Jaden said. "I guess that's almost as good as getting the money."

"Maybe better," Grace murmured. She liked the idea of doing something good for other people. It would be great to return a painting to relatives of the original owners. Imagine getting back a family heirloom that had disappeared so many years ago!

She just hoped they weren't getting in over their heads.

Too Many Riches

Grace and Jaden's parents were hesitant to let them take a train to Versailles. However, Sophie's mother convinced them that Sophie was capable of handling the train. As Dad said, "Kids grow up faster in big cities with good public transportation. Because of the subway system, kids who can't drive yet can get around on their own."

Mom glanced through the Paris guidebook with a sigh. "I'd love to have lunch at one of the tea rooms there." But fortunately for the kids, she had to work. It would be hard to hunt down Monsieur Dubois secretly with their mother in tow.

"We'll go another time," Dad promised. "But I have a deadline, and I think Joy might be getting a cold. I guess you kids are on your own. Stick together, and make sure you have the note with your address and phone number. And Jaden, don't touch anything unless Sophie says you can!"

They took a picnic lunch, which Sophie carried in a large tote bag. That would save them some money, since the entry fee was expensive. Sophie borrowed the guidebook and read from it on the train. "The site began as a hunting lodge. It was expanded into a palace. The royal court and the government of France moved to Versailles in 1682. Six thousand people lived there!"

"Wait, in one building?" Grace asked.

Sophie nodded. "It's a big building, kind of a U-shape with extra branches sticking out. Oh, and there are a couple of smaller palaces as well. They completely changed the landscape. They drained marshes, flattened hills, and moved forests."

"Why?" Jaden asked. "Forests and hills are cool! I'm not sure about that other thing you said."

"A marsh is land that is very wet," Sophie explained. "They put in gardens, ponds, and fountains. We will have to decide what we want to see. There's too much for one day."

"Let's just find Monsieur Dubois," Jaden said.

"No, we told your parents we were going to

Versailles, and they paid. We will see some of Versailles first. It is like eating your vegetables before you get dessert."

From the train station, they walked along a tree-lined path and then through a large parking lot. They crossed a broad cobblestone plaza to the palace grounds. First they wandered around the outside gardens. Everything was planted in straight rows or smooth curves, and neatly trimmed. Jets of water shot up from a large square pool. They saw round fountains and square fountains, spraying or trickling water. Some of the fountains had stone statues and one had statues colored gold. Small carts sold fresh orange juice, and a café offered sandwiches.

The morning got warmer, and the crowds got larger. The children had their picnic lunch in the garden before entering the palace itself.

"Why do we have to see another museum anyway?" Jaden asked. But when they got inside, his mouth dropped open and he stared at the amazing sights all around them. They wandered through rooms where every surface was decorated. Some walls were covered in ornate wallpaper with designs in velvet and gold trim. Other walls were of smooth stone, in different colors and patterns. The floors had patterns made of different colored wood, where they weren't covered with fancy carpets.

Elaborate paintings covered the ceilings. They showed gods, goddesses, and heroes from mythology. Huge paintings hung on the walls, with scenes from religion or history. They reminded Grace of the Rembrandt gallery at the Louvre. Maybe that was a good sign that their expert worked there someplace.

The Hall of Mirrors was bright with glittering chandeliers, their lights reflected in hundreds of mirrors. Even the furniture was fancy, sofas and chairs covered in patterned fabric, and tables with carved legs. Visitors crowded the palace as well, speaking many languages and posing for photos. Some listened to a tour on headphones, while large groups followed tour guides.

"It's kind of too much," Grace said after a while.

"Yeah." Jaden was holding Sophie's hand without complaint. "I'm afraid I'm going to bump something and break it and they'll charge me a million dollars!"

Sophie looked grim. "You can see why the people

revolted."

"Who did what?" Jaden asked.

Sophie waved a hand at the extravagant furniture. "Look how these people lived! They could spend money on painted ceilings and fancy clothes. They had the best food and drink, the best of everything. Meanwhile, ordinary people were starving." She glanced at the guidebook. "In 1789, the Revolutionaries attacked. They killed the palace guard. They dragged King Louis XVI and Queen Marie Antoinette back to Paris. There they were killed—beheaded."

Grace swallowed. "They cut off their heads? That's horrible. I mean, even if they had all the money that seems cruel."

"The rebels went too far," Sophie agreed. "Many nobles were killed in the years after the revolution. Ordinary people, too. One group took over, and then another. Each group killed the people who ruled before it, and anyone who disagreed with the new order. And then Napoleon, who started as a military hero, declared himself Emperor. He brought war across Europe."

Grace swallowed again. "What happened to him?"

"He too was defeated and went into exile."

"Where's that?" Jaden asked.

Sophie finally smiled. "Exile means he was sent away. He had to go live on an island so he wouldn't cause more trouble."

"That's better than being beheaded," Grace said.

"True." Sophie put the guidebook in her bag and offered a hand to each of the children. "Shall we leave this place and look for Monsieur Dubois?"

"How will we find him?" Grace asked. "This place is huge."

"Yes, 700 rooms, but Madame Estelle said he would be at the renovation workshop. That is where they restore art, cleaning it and making repairs. A good place to find a painting expert. The workshops are in the old stables."

They had a long walk to the stables, a large stone building that glowed golden in the afternoon light. "I thought these used to be stables for horses," Grace said. "It looks more like another palace."

"Even the horses lived better than the poor people," Sophie said. "These were the little stables."

She pointed at a sign on the stone wall that said "La Petites Ecuries." Grace knew la petites meant "the little." She had to trust Sophie for the meaning of ecuries, because the huge building looked more like a mansion than someplace to keep animals.

"There is another stable as well," Sophie said. "There they still have horses and do shows for the public."

"I'd like to see that," Grace said as they found the door to the building.

Inside, the stables looked more like a school, with tables and large lockers. Sophie spoke to several people in French before turning away with a frown. "No one knows Monsieur Dubois. They wonder if he may work at the ticket booth or café."

Grace frowned. "That doesn't sound like the expert we want."

"No. Either Madame Estelle made a mistake, or she gave us the wrong information on purpose." Sophie walked away from the building.

"I'm tired," Jaden said, dragging his feet as he trailed behind them. "I want to go home."

Sophie sighed. "Me, as well. Our trip was wasted."

"I liked the gardens," Grace said. "And the palace was interesting, just a lot to take in at once." They walked slowly toward the train. Grace's feet hurt, and she was getting hungry again. "Is there anything else to eat?"

"We have one chocolate bar I was saving for an emergency." Sophie moved to the side of the path and paused under a leafy tree. She slid her shoulder bag off her arm.

Grace caught a glimpse of movement from the corner of her eye. She turned as a large figure barreled toward them. Before she could move, the man pushed past her, knocked Sophie to the ground, and grabbed her bag.

Grace stared at the man's receding back, her heart racing with shock. Jaden yelled, "Hey, give that back!" and started after the man.

"Jaden, no!" Grace ran after him.

The man disappeared around the corner of a building. Jaden disappeared after him.

7

More Mysteries

Grace and Sophie heard a shout. By the time Grace reached the building she was panting for breath. She swung around the corner and skidded to a stop. The man was disappearing into the distance, but Jaden stood only a few feet away. Sophie's bag lay at his feet, her belongings scattered.

Grace crossed the last few feet to Jaden. Sophie ran up to them a second later. "What happened?"

Jaden said, "When I got to the corner, he had stopped. He turned the bag upside down, dumped everything on the ground, and ran away. I didn't catch him, but I got your stuff back."

Sophie hugged him. "I'm glad you did not catch him. Chasing him was dangerous and foolish. You are a brave little man but you scared me half to death."

Jaden squirmed out of her grasp. "If I'd caught him, we could have put him in jail."

"He was twice your size," Grace said. "I'm just glad you're not hurt. Sophie, are you all right?"

"A little bruised on my bottom, but I have both of you, and I have my bag, so I am well." She crouched and began gathering her things. "It's a strange thief who leaves the wallet. You must have startled him before he finished his search."

"Should we call the police?" Grace asked.

Sophie picked up her phone. The screen was cracked. "Not on this. He got nothing, yet still managed to destroy my poor phone." She sat on the ground, peeled the paper back from a chocolate bar, and offered them pieces. "I don't know what the

police could do. The man is long gone. Did either of you get a good look at him?"

"He was tall and had dark hair." Grace frowned. "There was something familiar about him but I can't think what."

"He had on a hat and sunglasses and a dark jacket," Jaden said.

"Yes," Sophie agreed. "That made it hard to see his face, but easy to change how he looks. By now he has taken off the hat and glasses and blended into the crowds." She nibbled chocolate for a while. "It is a strange theft. Pickpockets are common wherever tourists are. They work among the crowds, plucking wallets from pockets or cutting purse straps. But they disappear before you know you've been robbed."

"But this is the first time today we haven't been in a big crowd," Grace said. "And there was nothing secret about the way he knocked into you."

Sophie nodded. "He called attention to himself, and yet he didn't take anything. What does that mean?"

Grace looked around nervously. "Let's get out of here."

Sophie rose and slung her bag back over her shoulder. "I agree. We'll mention the thief at the ticket office, but I don't think the police will do anything."

They reported the attack and borrowed a phone to warn their parents they would be late. Then they walked to the station and waited for the train. When they finally boarded the train, Sophie leaned back and closed her eyes. "What a long day."

Jaden slumped in his seat. "I'm hungry."

"Me too," Grace said. "We have a half hour on the train, though."

"And no more chocolate!" Sophie moaned.

They rode in silence. Grace's eyes closed and her head started to nod. She jolted back awake before she tipped over. She rubbed her face and glanced around. A dozen other people sat scattered around the car. She amused herself for a few minutes by studying them and wondering where they were going.

At the far end of the car, a tall man sat hunched with his back to them. He wore a dark jacket and hat. A chill ran down Grace's spine. It was probably only a coincidence. Lots of tall men wore dark clothes, and the thief had no reason to follow them.

She had to make sure. She glanced at Sophie and Jaden, who were half asleep. Grace rose and crept down the aisle. Could she get a better look at the man without him seeing her?

She stopped several feet behind the man. The window beside him reflected his face in profile. Grace gasped. She recognized him!

She hurried back to Sophie and Jaden and shook them awake. "The man from the gallery! The one who was in the back room, who came out after we left. He's on this train. And I think he was the thief!" Grace pointed him out.

The train pulled into a station. "Don't look at him now!" Sophie warned. "Here's where we change to the Metro. We'll see if he follows us."

They tried to act natural as they exited the train and switched to the subway. When they found seats, Sophie kept her face turned one way while her eyes looked another. As the Metro rumbled forward, she said, "He came in behind us and he's hiding again."

"What does it all mean?" Grace whispered.

Sophie thought for a while. "It begins to make sense. Madame Estelle sends us to find a man who does not exist. She also sends her employee to steal my bag. She must have hoped we had the painting with us."

"But if it's not valuable ..." Grace stopped. "You mean she thinks it's a real Rembrandt?"

Sophie grinned. "This is not proof, but it seems Madame Estelle was willing to take a chance. When we would not sell it cheaply, and would not tell her where we lived, she came up with this plan."

Jaden's eyes were wide. "This is so cool!"

"She is clever," Sophie said. "If the man had succeeded in stealing the painting, who would believe we ever had it? She would say we are merely imaginative children."

"But what do we do now?" Grace asked.

Sophie pulled out her phone, but it would not turn on. "We cannot call ahead to have the police waiting. We could try to find a guard at the station, but the man will disappear while we explain. No matter, we know where he works. We must go home and tell our parents everything now. It has become dangerous. But I'm afraid that man may be hoping to follow us home. I would rather he not find out where we live."

Grace shuddered. "Me too."

"So we will get off at a different station and elude him."

"Do what to him?" Jaden asked.

Sophie smiled. "We will be like the movie heroes and escape from him. We will get away and hide, and then take the Metro home when we are sure he is not following."

"Where should we get off?" Grace asked.

Sophie looked at the subway map. "I know the perfect place to hide from an enemy. The cemetery!"

CREEPY
WEEPING WOMEN

8

"We must be ready to leave the train," Sophie said. "But do not look like you are ready! Let other people get off, and then we will run through the doors. Maybe he won't be quick enough to follow us."

"Are we really going to a cemetery?" Grace asked.

"Yeah, cool!" Jaden said.

"Shh," Sophie whispered, "Cimitière du Père Lachaise is large and beautiful, like a park. Many people come to visit the graves of famous people. Musicians, writers, artists, all are buried there. This is the stop. Be ready!"

Grace tried not to look at the man from the gallery. From the edge of her vision, she saw him turn to watch them as the subway car stopped. A few people got off and a couple more got on. "Now!" Sophie grabbed their hands and they ran for the door. Grace tripped over another passenger's foot and stumbled. Jaden shot through the door. It started to close between them.

Sophie stopped in the door and leaned her shoulder against it. Grace took the last few steps through it and it closed behind them.

Jaden waved them forward. "He got off too!"

Grace glanced down the subway platform. The thief had gotten through the far door. She followed Sophie and Jaden as they raced through the station.

They exited into a dimly lit street. Night was falling. They ran toward a large stone wall and through a wide opening in it. "Off the main path," Sophie said. They darted to the left among the trees and tombs. But these were not merely gravestones. They had to squeeze between monuments that rose taller than a person. Stone statues of angels and weeping women surrounded them. The graves were so close together that they had to crawl over some of the lower stone markers.

After a few minutes, they huddled against a stone wall. "Perhaps we have lost him," Sophie whispered. They waited in silence, listening for sounds of pursuit. The cemetery was eerily quiet. Grace couldn't remember seeing anyone else in there. She brushed a strand of hair from her face and her hand grazed the wall. It felt oddly soft, like velvet. She stroked her fingers down the stone and realized it was covered with moss. In the fading light she could barely make out the green color.

A piece of the wall seemed to shift under her gaze. Grace almost yelped as a face appeared in the stone. She stared, willing it to disappear. It had to be her imagination.

The face remained, a man with deep-set eyes and a mustache. Grace nudged Jaden and pointed.

He turned toward the wall and his eyes opened wide. "Cool!" he whispered. "The wall has faces."

So it wasn't her imagination. Grace shifted back for a better view of the wall and saw a line of faces. For some reason they had been carved into the stone blocks. Creepy!

"Hush!" Sophie put an arm around each of them and pulled them down to crouch against the wall. Footsteps rang on the stone path. The steps paused, as if the person was scanning the area and listening. Grace tried to breathe quietly. Her legs started to hurt from her crouched position, but she didn't dare move.

Finally the footsteps moved on. Several more minutes passed. Finally Sophie rose. She shook her leg and muttered, "I have ants on my leg."

"Oh no." Grace backed away and brushed at her own legs.

Sophie chuckled. "It is an expression, a what-do-you-call-it? An idiom. I have stayed in one position too long, and my foot feels funny. Tingly, as if ants are crawling on it."

Grace straightened. "Oh. We say our foot fell asleep."

"Strange," Sophie said. "Let's see if our path is safe."

"If the coast is clear," Jaden said.

Sophie frowned. "But we are not on the coast."

They crept slowly toward the path. They didn't spot the thief or anyone else. They headed back the way they had come. The footsteps had gone in the opposite direction.

They reached the gate. It was closed. Sophie pushed on it but it was locked tightly. The high walls on either side were topped with spikes. They backed away from the gate and looked around. Sophie said, "I forgot they close the cemetery at night. Do you have a saying for when you are in trouble and don't know what to do? In French we say it is to be like a chicken who has found a knife—useless. Also, we do not know on which foot to dance."

Grace considered. "We might say up a creek without a paddle. I guess it means you're in a boat and don't have any way to row to shore." That seemed to sum up their situation. Sophie's phone was broken. They were locked inside the cemetery alone. Or worse, maybe the thief was locked in with them.

"There are doors in some of these stone buildings," Jaden said.

"Those are tombs," Sophie explained. "Nothing inside except dead bodies."

"Oh." Jaden considered. "Maybe we could spend the night in one if we can't get out of here."

"I am not spending the night in a tomb!" Grace said.

Jaden grinned at her. "What's the problem if you don't believe in ghosts?"

"I don't. Still, it's probably cold and damp and yucky in there."

Sophie put her hands on her hips and looked around. "Well, we will not be like a wet chicken and comb the giraffe!"

Jaden chuckled. "What does that mean?" Grace asked.

"A wet chicken is a coward. Combing the giraffe means doing something useless." Sophie gestured to the graves around them. "We will pass by these people who are sucking the dandelions by the root. We had our feathers hot, but we will find a way out of this danger. There are other exits. Maybe one will be open."

It was scary walking through the dark, lonely cemetery at night. But at least they were together. Sophie talked softly to keep up their mood. But anytime they heard a strange noise, they froze, listening for the thief.

9

Trapped Among the Tombs!

"What do you think that man will do if he finds us?" Grace asked. "He knows we don't have the painting with us. What does he want?"

"Most likely he will try to follow us again in secret. We must watch out for him." Sophie led the way around a stone tomb the size of a garden shed. Next to the fancy metal door stood a statue of someone draped in a robe. Grace couldn't get used to all the stone people scattered around the cemetery. She kept waiting for one to lunge at her.

"However..." Sophie hesitated. "There is a chance he wants to capture us and make us take him to the painting. If he tries, you must run. He cannot hold all three of us. Even if he captures me, do not return. Find the police and have them call your parents to warn them. You have your phone number?"

Grace and Jaden nodded. They edged closer to

Sophie. "You're very brave," Grace said.

Sophie smiled. "I have always enjoyed the spy stories, the mysteries. Perhaps I will become a police investigator."

"Me too," Jaden said.

"Not me," Grace said. "But if I have to be lost in a cemetery at night, I'm glad I'm with you two."

They reached another exit, but that door was also closed and bolted. A few people passed by on the street outside. Sophie called to them, trying to get their attention without yelling too loudly. "Au secours, s'il vous plait! Help us please!"

One or two glanced over but continued on. Sophie sighed. "They would not be able to unlock the door anyway. I suppose we are not the first to be trapped here, so perhaps they have seen this before. They probably think we are foolish tourists and deserve what we get for not knowing the closing time. But there must be an exit somewhere for those foolish tourists!"

They kept going, half stumbling in the dark. Lights from the city spilled over the tops of the walls, but inside the cemetery the ground was in deep shadow.

A stray beam from a streetlight glowed on a greenish figure. A man was climbing out of a hole between some boulders! Grace gasped and stared. For a moment the man wavered as if moving. But no, it was only her imagination, or her own trembling. It was another statue, tinted green from years of exposure to the rain. Why would someone make a statue of a man trapped among the rough rocks?

The third door was also closed and locked.

The statues loomed grimly, caught among gray light and black shadows. Grace wished she had a flashlight, although that would have made it easier for the thief to spot them. They scrambled over a stone marker in the shape of a coffin. Grace tried not to think about the thousands of dead people all around them.

"Look!" Jaden exclaimed. "There are no spikes on the wall here."

They stared up at the top of the wall. Even without spikes on top, it would not be easy to get over. The wall rose high above their heads, higher than they could reach with their arms stretched up. "There are trees on the other side," Sophie said. "If we get to the top, and can reach a tree, that might be a way down. I can boost you two up."

"But what about you?" Grace asked. No one would be left to boost Sophie, and Grace didn't think she or Jaden could pull Sophie up from the top. Grace wasn't at all certain she could get down a tree on the other side either. "Maybe this isn't such a good idea."

Sophie backed up from the wall, studying it. "I might be able to jump." She moved closer and ran her hands over the stones. "This block has crumbled enough to leave a little edge. If I can jump to it with my foot and push off, I think I can get my arms on top of the wall."

"Can I try that too?" Jaden asked.

Sophie chuckled. "You may not have enough experience with gymnastics. Also, I am taller. Don't pout, it will be enough of an adventure getting over the wall. You must go first and help your sister." Sophie winked at Grace, who nodded. Sophie might be trying to humor Jaden, but Grace would be happy for help, even from her little brother. She did not have his comfort with heights.

Sophie crouched down. "Climb onto my

shoulders," she told Jaden. He straddled her neck and she slowly stood. "Now you must stand up on my shoulders. Put your hands against the wall for balance."

Grace got behind Sophie and held her arms out loosely. That was the way Sophie had taught them to spot someone in gymnastics. If Jaden fell, Grace wouldn't try to catch him. He would be too heavy for that and they both might get hurt. But she would soften his fall and try to keep his head from hitting the ground.

Sophie braced herself against the wall while Jaden wriggled from sitting on her shoulders to standing. She held onto his legs. "Can you reach the top?"

"I can touch it, but I don't think I can pull myself up."

"Good thing you don't weigh much," Sophie said. "I'm going to grab your feet and push you up." She wriggled her hands underneath Jaden's feet. "You remember your French numbers? On trois. Un, deux, trois!" Sophie straightened her arms and lifted Jaden high enough that he could flop onto the top of the wall on his stomach. "You are all right?"

"No problem!" He shifted to straddle the wall and sat up.

"Good." Sophie crouched again. "Your turn, Grace."

Grace looked up at the top of the wall. Jaden grinned at her. "Come on, it's fun."

She glanced around the dark cemetery. Climbing over the wall was probably more fun than spending the night surrounded by a bunch of tombs. Grace took a deep breath and climbed onto Sophie's shoulders. Sophie shifted her weight and slowly stood. Grace wobbled then pressed her hands against the wall for balance.

"All right, up you go," Sophie said. "And when we get to the other side, the first thing I'm going to do is buy us each a chocolate bar to celebrate."

Grace managed to smile, but it faded quickly as she tried to shift from sitting to standing. It wasn't easy to get a foot up on Sophie's shoulder. They both did some grunting and wobbling before Grace managed it.

Finally she stood, with Sophie's hands on her calves and her own hands on top of the wall. "Can you reach it from here?" Sophie asked.

The wall was just under Grace's chin. She could reach her arms over it, but getting her whole body up would be harder. She didn't think she was strong enough to pull herself all the way up. Jaden straddled the wall beside her. He patted her arm. "Come on, you can do it."

Grace wanted to snap at him. This wasn't easy for her like it was for him! This wasn't fun, it was scary! But he was trying to be helpful. That was rare enough that she should appreciate it. She forced herself to smile. "A little extra boost would help."

"All right." Sophie's hands moved under Grace's feet. "Count with me. Un, deux, trois!"

Grace counted along, and on trois she pushed with her arms as Sophie pushed against her feet. Grace flopped on top of the wall, her head hanging off one side and her feet hanging off the other. For a moment she thought she was going to somersault down the other side. But Sophie held onto her feet and Jaden grabbed her shoulder.

When Grace recovered her breath, she drew one leg over the wall and turned sideways to straddle it.

"How does it look for getting down?" Sophie asked.

Grace groaned. After all that work, she didn't want to go anywhere! But she couldn't spend the night on top of a wall. She looked over into the street. It was surprisingly empty, with no cars driving past. She spotted only a few people walking in the distance. That was probably good, so no one would ask what they were doing. Trees grew close to the wall. "I think this tree is close enough. It looks sturdy."

Jaden was already reaching for a nearby branch.

"Good, wait for me so I can spot you ..." Before Sophie finished her sentence, Jaden was scrambling down the tree trunk. The doctors said his hearing was fine, but somehow he didn't hear orders unless the person was looking him in the eye. He was like an ostrich that thought it was invisible if it couldn't see anyone. Only with Jaden, if he wasn't looking at you, he could pretend not to hear you.

"Too late," Grace called down to Sophie.

The French girl shook her head. "Take this." Sophie handed up her bag. "Move over a little, so I can get up." She backed away from the wall as Grace inched herself along it.

Sophie backed up, ran at the wall, and jumped. Her foot touched it, and then her hands reached the top. But she fell back down, landing on her feet and rolling onto her back. "Oof, not quite." Sophie stood up, brushing herself off. "I will get it this time."

"You were close," Grace said.

A sudden yell startled Grace so much she almost fell off the wall. She whipped her head around to stare down at Jaden. "Let go of me!" he shouted, trying to pull away from the man who had a hold of his arm.

It was the gallery thief. A few feet away, Madame Estelle stood smiling.

To the Rescue

10

Jaden kicked the man in the shins. The thief grunted but didn't let go. Madame Estelle said something in French and gestured down the street. The man started dragging Jaden away. Were they kidnapping him? They must be hoping to trade Jaden for the painting!

Grace didn't have time to be afraid. She didn't even have time to think. She had to help her brother.

She reached out for the tree branch and hauled herself onto it. Leaves slapped her in the face as she crawled toward the trunk. She worked her way down the tree, balancing on branches that shook under her feet. The rough bark bit into her palms. She focused only on the next step down.

Suddenly she was on the ground. She spun away from the tree and ran after Jaden. The man had picked him up around the waist and was carrying

him. Jaden was still struggling, squirming and wriggling and lashing out at anything he could hit. It was slowing the man down, but not stopping him.

Madame Estelle reached a car and opened the door. She yelled something and waved to the man to hurry.

Grace's feet pounded the pavement. She heard yelling, as if from a great distance. Sound seemed muffled and she was moving in slow motion.

Jaden landed a kick on the man's knee. The thief yelped and almost let go, but before Jaden could pull away, the man hauled him back up. They were still a few steps from the car. Grace was almost there.

She barreled straight into the man. Then they were tumbling, his coat flapping in her face, blinding her.

The three of them landed on the ground in a heap.

Grace sat up, shaking hair out of her face. Her ears were ringing and the ground seemed to be moving. Jaden jumped up beside her and held out a hand. "Come on!"

Something was moving underneath her—she was sitting on the man's stomach. He groaned as she scrambled to her feet. Sophie raced toward them, screaming, "Au secours! Police!" Jaden and Grace ran to her.

The three of them came together. Grace glanced back. Madame Estelle stood by the car, staring at them. The man lay on the ground moaning. A few other people were drawing closer. A woman speaking on a cell phone hurried up to them and nodded at Sophie. She said something in French that included the word "police."

Madame Estelle got in the car and drove away. A police siren drew closer.

Sophie hugged Grace and Jaden close. "A chocolate bar is not enough today. We need gâteau au chocolat. We deserve an entire chocolate cake each!"

Memories

11

The thief quickly blamed Madame Estelle for the plan to steal the painting. The police picked her up at her gallery. The two would not cause any more trouble.

It was late before Sophie, Grace and Jaden got to go home. They'd had to explain everything to the police, and to their parents. They were scolded for keeping the painting secret. At least the adults agreed that no one could have predicted the danger that would result. And everyone was excited to see the painting. But was it a real Rembrandt?

Finding out took weeks of testing. Experts studied the art style and the initials. They tested the paint and canvas to see how old it was. They x-rayed the painting to look at the layers of paint. That helped determine the painting's age, and they also learned more about the artist's style. Finally the verdict came in. It was a real Rembrandt!

During that time, Mom and her history colleagues researched the families that hid in the attic. One family died in the Nazi camps. But the other had two children who survived. One of those children was still alive! She was an elderly woman living in New York City. She had children, grandchildren and great-grandchildren. The woman remembered a painting that hung in her house when she was a child. She described the portrait of a woman, and it matched the painting from the attic. That helped prove the painting belonged to her family.

It turned out the laws were strange when it came to returning art stolen by the Nazis. Often current owners could keep the art, no matter how they'd gotten it. But the woman who owned the house was happy to return the painting. She'd been a young child during the war, but she remembered the horrors. She wanted the painting to go to its rightful owners.

They returned the painting at a big ceremony. Sophie, Grace, and Jaden got to meet the woman who'd hidden in the attic so many years ago. She cried when she got her painting back. "I have nothing from before the war," she said. "No family pictures, no heirlooms. Until now. You have returned a great treasure."

"It's worth a lot of money," Jaden said.

"It's worth more than money," the woman said. "It's family history."

After the ceremony, Sophie and her mother joined Grace's family at their house. Grace's dad baked a huge chocolate cake. As they ate, Grace asked, "Do we have any family heirlooms?"

Mom and Dad thought about it. "We have a lot of photos," Mom said. "And I have some jewelry from my grandmother that you kids will get one day."

"We have some souvenirs from our trip to China," Dad said. "I don't know if they're old enough to be family heirlooms yet. But one day you may treasure them because of the memories."

"The memories are valuable," Sophie said. "That woman did not care how much the painting was worth. She loved it because it reminded her of her childhood."

"It's the people who matter," Mom said. "But the stories, and the objects that remind us of the stories, help us remember the people."

Grace took another bite of the gooey chocolate cake. "I'll remember the story of finding this painting for a long time."

Jaden grinned. "I'll remember you tackling that guy!"

Mom rose. "That reminds me, I have something for you all." She opened the box sitting on the counter and pulled out three framed pictures. They were all the same—the portrait of a woman by Rembrandt. "They're photographs," Mom said. "One for each of you kids, so you can remember this summer, and the time you found a piece of history."

Sophie took hers and hugged it to her chest. "I will treasure it always, as a reminder of my dear American friends."

"I'll look at it and remember you," Grace said. "And how much fun we had finding out about it, even if I was scared sometimes."

"I'll remember I once held something worth millions of dollars!" Jaden said.

They all laughed. One way or another, it was a summer to remember.

Grace's Travel Journal

Lots of people in France speak some English. They like it if you at least try to speak a little French, though. Many Americans think they'll be understood if they just speak English loudly. Then the French like to pretend they don't understand a word you're saying. Learn to say a few words, such as bonjour (hello) and merci (thank you).

People dress up a lot more in Paris. They don't wear jeans or tennis shoes to restaurants. They don't wear shorts and flip-flops except at the beach. Instead, they wear chic, or stylish, clothing and jewelry.

Friends often greet each other with a kiss on each cheek.

Everyone in Paris goes on vacation in August. Even the restaurants are closed. It's hot and humid, so people head to the mountains or the beach.

They really do eat French fries in France! They're called pommes frites.

Roasted Chicken, Apples, and Leeks Recipe

Prep Time: about 15 minutes
Total Time: about one hour
Serves 4

4 small crisp apples (such as Fuji, Honeycrisp,
    Empire or Braeburn)
2 leeks
6 small sprigs of fresh rosemary
2 tablespoons olive oil
1 teaspoon kosher salt, divided
1 teaspoon black pepper, divided
4 small chicken thighs and 4 drumsticks (about 2 1/2
    pounds total)

1. Heat oven to 400 degrees Fahrenheit. Ask an
    adult to help you with the hot oven and sharp
    knives.

2. Cut off and discard the roots and dark green
    tops of the leeks. Cut the remaining white
    and light green parts in half crosswise. Cut those
    sections in half lengthwise. Rinse well and cold
    water.

3. Cut the apple into thick slices, discarding the
    core.

4. In a large roasting pan, mix the apples, leeks,
    rosemary, olive oil, and half the salt and pepper.

5. Sprinkle the chicken pieces with the remaining
    1/2 teaspoon each of salt and pepper. Place the
    chicken skin-side up among the vegetables.

6. Roast 40 to 45 minutes, until the apples and
    leeks are tender. Make sure the chicken is
    cooked through.

Country Facts

Capital: Paris

Language: French

Population: About 63 million in mainland France. France also oversees French Guiana in South America, and the islands of Guadeloupe, Martinique, Mayotte, and Reunion. These overseas regions bring the population to over 66 million.

Climate: Mild summers and cool winters inland. Mild winters and hot summers along the Mediterranean coast.

Famous people:
Claude Monet, painter (1840 - 1926): Monet was one of the painters who started the Impressionist movement. Before them, most European painters tried to make their paintings look exactly like the subject. The Impressionists used strong colors and brushstrokes you could see. This gives an impression of the subject, instead of a perfect copy.

Louis XVI, King (1754 - 1793): Born in the Palace of Versailles, Louis became King of France in 1774. The country was in turmoil, and Louis resisted change. He was accused of treason and sentenced to death during the French Revolution.

Joan of Arc (1412 - 1431): Joan was from a poor peasant family. She started having visions at age 12. England had invaded France. Joan convinced the French leader to fight the English. She led an army into battle when she was 17 years old. She was captured and killed, but remained an inspiration. She is now the patron saint of France.

Events and Holidays

Fete de la Federation, on July 14, is sometimes called Bastille Day. The Bastille, a prison, was captured by a mob of rebels in 1789. This signaled the start of the French Revolution. The anniversary is celebrated with parades, speeches, and fireworks. It's a lot like the Fourth of July in America!

Victory in Europe Day is May 8. VE Day marks the official end of World War II.

Many religious holidays are also celebrated. These include Noel (Christmas) on December 25, and Pâques (Easter Sunday) in March or April. All Saints Day on November 1 celebrates all the Christian saints.

Landmarks

Eiffel Tower: Gustave Eiffel built this tower for the 1889 World's Fair. It was the tallest building in the world at the time—1,063 feet high! It was a symbol of the modern age, and some Parisians thought it was ugly. The tower was supposed to be torn down in 1909. Instead, it became a popular symbol of France.

Louvre: Once a fortress, then a royal palace, it is now the world's biggest museum. It holds 35,000 works of art. It would take nine months just to glance at every piece.

Palace of Versailles: A 700-room palace that could house 6,000 people. The grounds include gardens, ponds, canals, and fountains. It was the seat of the royal court from 1682 until 1789. Now it's a museum.

Cemetery of Père-Lachaise: Over a million people are buried in this Paris cemetery. It's known for elaborate tombs and famous dead people.

Now and Then

The Eiffel Tower was built as a tourist attraction. It still is one. It hasn't changed a lot, but there are some differences. In 1889, a light in the bell tower swung around with a blue, white, and red signal. Now the tower is lit up by thousands of lights at night. In 1890, almost 400,000 people visited the tower. Now almost seven million people visit each year!

Georges Garen's painting of the illumination of the Eiffel Tower during the Exposition in 1889.

Discussion Questions

1. What makes something valuable? Is it what the thing is, how old it is, who made it, how rare it is, or something else?

2. What kind of objects might be considered heirlooms? Why are family heirlooms important to people?

3. Do you have photos or objects that help you remember special people or events?

4. If you find something valuable, should you try to return it to its owner, or do you believe in "finders keepers"?

5. In chapter five, Sophie says, "But if we find out the truth, we can help right a wrong from the past." Is it possible to make up for past crimes or mistakes?

6. If some people control all the money, should poor people rebel? Why or why not?

7. In chapter eight, Sophie and Grace share some idioms. These are expressions that mean something different from the literal meaning of the words. Can you think of some more idioms? How is their meaning different from the actual words?

Vocabulary

Do you know these words? Try using each in a sentence.

commemorate	locals
elude	mime
euros	monument
exile	portrait
expert	rebel
extravagant	renovate
forgery	restore
heirlooms	revolt
idiom	signature
initials	traditional

Websites to Visit

Learn more about the landmarks, historic events, and people of France:

http://kids.nationalgeographic.com/content/kids/en_US/explore/countries/france

www.kids-world-travel-guide.com/france-facts.html

www.timeforkids.com/destination/france/history-timeline

About the Author:

M. M. Eboch writes fiction and nonfiction for all ages. Writing as Chris Eboch, her novels for young people include *The Genie's Gift*, a middle eastern fantasy; *The Eyes of Pharaoh*, a mystery in ancient Egypt; *The Well of Sacrifice*, a Mayan adventure; *Bandits Peak*, a survival story; and the Haunted  series, which starts with *The Ghost on the Stairs*. As M. M. Eboch, her books include nonfiction and the fictionalized biographies *Jesse Owens: Young Record Breaker* and *Milton Hershey: Young Chocolatier*. Learn more at www.chriseboch.com.

About the Illustrator:

Sarah Horne studied illustration at Falmouth College of Arts, England, graduating in 2001. Sarah now specializes in funny inky illustration and text for young fiction and picture books. She also works on book covers, magazine and newspaper editorials and in Advertising. She loves music,  painting, color, photography, film, scratchy jazz and a good cup of coffee.

Sarah lives on a hill in London, UK.